# Dear Parent:
## Your child's love of readinç

D0485255

Every child learns to read in a different way and at his or her own speed. You can help your young reader improve and become more confident by encouraging his or her own interests and abilities. You can also guide your child's spiritual development by reading stories with biblical values and Bible stories, like I Can Read! books published by Zonderkidz. From books your child reads with you to the first books he or she reads alone, there are I Can Read! books for every stage of reading:

**SHARED READING**
Basic language, word repetition, and whimsical illustrations, Ideal for sharing with your emergent reader.

**BEGINNING READING**
Short sentences, familiar words, and simple concepts for children eager to read on their own.

**READING WITH HELP**
Engaging stories, longer sentences, and language play for developing readers.

**READING ALONE**
Complex plots, challenging vocabulary, and high-interest topics for the independent reader.

**ADVANCED READING**
Short paragraphs, chapters, and exciting themes for the perfect bridge to chapter books.

**I Can Read!** books have introduced children to the joy of reading since 1957. Featuring award-winning authors and illustrators and a fabulous cast of beloved characters, I Can Read! books set the standard for beginning readers.

A lifetime of discovery begins with the magical words "I Can Read!"

*Visit www.icanread.com for information on enriching your child's reading experience.*
*Visit www.zonderkidz.com for more Zonderkidz I Can Read! titles.*

"Which of the three do you think was a neighbor
to the man who was attacked by robbers?"
—*Luke 10:36*

ZONDERKIDZ

*Princess Charity's Golden Heart*
Copyright © 2012 by Zonderkidz

Requests for information should be addressed to:

Zonderkidz, 5300 Patterson Ave. SE, Grand Rapids, Michigan 49530

ISBN 978-0-310-73248-8

Editor: Mary Hassinger
Design: Diane Mielke

Printed in China

12 13 14 15 16 17 /DSC/ 7 6 5 4 3 2 1

# I Can Read!

BEGINNING
1
READING

The Princess Parables™

# Princess Charity's Golden Heart

Story inspired by **Jeanna Young** & **Jacqueline Johnson**
Pictures by **Omar Aranda**

Princess Charity lived in a castle.

She had four sisters.

They are Joy, Faith, Grace,

and Hope.

Their daddy is the king.

Princess Charity was the

youngest princess.

She liked to run and play.

She liked adventure.

One day, Princess Charity

went to the barn.

She took care of her horse, Daisy.

Then she wanted to go for a ride.

"Where are you going today?"

asked her friend Harry.

"I will not go far, Harry," said Charity.

"I will not go to Sir Richard's land."

Princess Charity hugged Daisy's nose.

Daisy was a special gift from God.

That night the king told his princesses many stories.

The girls loved to hear about their daddy's trips.

Princess Charity wanted to go with the king someday.

Charity spoke up,

"Daddy, why can't I go with you?

I want to go past the Weeping Woodlands."

The king said, "No, Charity.

That is Sir Richard's land.

You cannot go there.

Do you all understand?"

The next day, Charity packed a lunch.

She left a note to tell her sisters

she went riding.

She went to the stable to get Daisy.

Princess Charity rode to a big hill.

She looked at the kingdom.

She looked past Weeping Woodlands

to Sir Richard's land.

While Charity was eating lunch
she saw a young boy in a buggy.

*He is going too fast*, Charity thought.

*He is too close to Sir Richard's land!*

Then the buggy's wheel broke!

The boy fell out of the buggy.

Princess Charity prayed,

"How can I help that boy, God?"

Charity saw something coming.

It was a fancy coach.

"They will help the boy,"

Charity said to Daisy.

But the coach drove away.

Charity jumped on Daisy.

She rode close to the hurt boy.

Then Charity saw some of Sir

Richard's men coming.

"Thank you, Lord!" Princess Charity said.

"I know they will help."

But just like the fancy coach,

they rode away and did not help.

Princess Charity knew

she had to help the boy.

She knew he was on Sir Richard's land.

The king might get upset.

But Charity helped the boy.

She helped him get into the cart.

She took him to the castle.

The princess sisters saw Charity
and the boy in the cart.

"Who is he?" asked Faith

"Can we help too?" asked Grace.

The king asked Charity,

"Where did you find the boy?"

"Daddy, I was near Sir Richard's land.

I saw him get hurt.

I had to help!" she said.

Then they heard horses coming to

the castle.

Sir Richard was at the castle.

"Is my son here?" he asked the king.

"Yes, Princess Charity saw him get hurt.

She helped him."

Sir Richard said,

"Princess, you are a good neighbor.

You are a good friend.

I thank God for you and your kindness.

How can I show my thanks?"

Later, the king said,

"I am proud of you, Charity.

You were a good neighbor to

Sir Richard's son.

Thanks to you, our kingdoms will have

peace together again."